TreeSong

H.E. Stewart

Library and Archives Canada Cataloguing in Publication

Stewart, H. E. (Helen Elizabeth), 1943–

TreeSong / H.E. Stewart.

ISBN 978-0-9693852-6-4

I. Title.

PS8587.T4855T74 2010   jC813'.54   C2010-901305-0

Manufactured by Friesens Corporation in
Altona, Manitoba, in April 2010, Job #51223

PRINTED IN CANADA

Tudor House Press is committed to reducing the consumption of ancient forests.
This book is one step towards that goal. It is printed on acid-free paper that is
100% ancient forest free, and has been processed chlorine free.

for Isabel Magaña

my very dear piano teacher, who taught me
that the practice of any art can be like prayer

and for Gerry Illmayer

whose healing hands help to make my work possible

Long eons ago, lost in a changing mist of forgotten time, all the Earth was blanketed in a grandeur of green. Down through many ancient ages, silent forests darkened every mountainside and hillside of the Pacific Northwest.

In the vastness of the universe, our small blue world followed its course, always turning toward the morning. Seasons came and went. Sun warmed the Earth, fog rose from the oceans, clouds gathered, spilling rain. Winter snow drifted down over the forests and mountains, then melted away as the world turned once again to greening and growing.

This was an old, old pattern, ancient beyond all memory and dreaming. Over endless seasons, plant life grew and died, and grew again.

Decaying leaves and fallen debris piled layer
upon layer, slowly crumbling and collecting
into soil. This rich beautiful topsoil, thousands
of years in the making, nurtures all that grows.

Ferns opened like feathered stars. Mosses spread in waves of spongy brightness over the forest floor carrying a strange enchantment into the darkness of growing trees. This was a time when the land was home to bear and deer, the sky was filled with birds and the sea with salmon.

For centuries the First Nations People depended on this abundance
for all their needs. They honoured the land, the sea, and the wild life.
They were part of this world and understood its spirit. This was their
home. Many could hear the singing of the trees.

Millions of tiny seeds fell from these trees and scattered over the deep-cushioned moss. A few landed on fallen rotting wood that provided nourishment and a place to take hold. This is where our tiny Sitka spruce began its life, long before Europeans first settled in North America.

In the forest-green shade, the seedling grew slowly, hardly noticeable during its first years. Always reaching towards the light, the little spruce after a decade was taller than a man. After fifty years, it was forty feet tall and home to many birds, as well as myriads of beetles and bugs. After two centuries the tree was almost three hundred feet tall, one of the tallest in a forest of tall trees. It was part of a living community, home to birds and insects, to fungi and ferns, lichens and moss. The tree was important to the whole forest as the forest is important to the whole world.

With each new morning, the first delicate light of dawn fell onto the mountain peaks and then onto the topmost branches of the tall tree. As the day warmed, the tree gathered in the sun's energy, while its deep roots drew moisture and food from the earth. When evening settled quietly over the land, the last rays of setting sun lit the tree top, for a moment turning its cones to ornaments of hammered gold, a wonder known only to the eagle.

The tree had lived for countless seasons, endless days and
nights. It had watched over the forest as winter storms turned to
gentle spring rains. It had held the night sky bright with stars high
within its branches, then had turned to silver as the moon moved
across the heavens, spilling light down onto the earth below.

The Sitka spruce
had become part
of the landscape,
connecting the
Earth to the heavens
and one generation to
the next. So old and
strong, this tree seemed
part of time itself.

The tree stood under the long curve of silent sky as gathering clouds drifted by, piling higher and growing darker. Rain began to fall, first in heavy single drops, then in a drenching downpour, washing the sky and all the forest. Water trickled down through the trees, dripping from every tiny branch, dropping at last to soak into the soil.

When the skies cleared, the trees were shining, the birds singing, and the air as fresh and sweet as when time began.

Each day was different, but the pattern of forest life continued unbroken. And always every part of creation was linked to every other.

Then the first Europeans arrived in North America, and the old, unchanging pattern was forever changed. These settlers took the land and claimed it as their own. With immense effort, they set about creating homesteads for themselves. They cut and burned the trees, then ploughed the land, forcing out native wildlife and the First Nations People who depended upon the plants and animals for food and medicine.

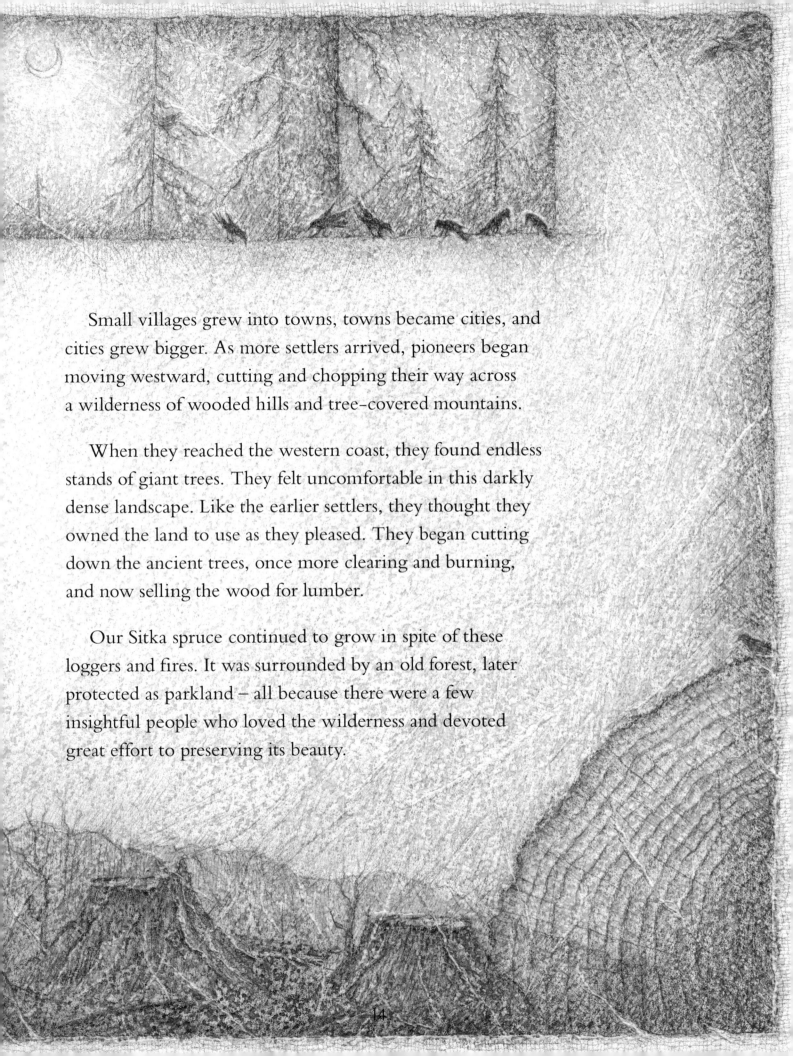

Small villages grew into towns, towns became cities, and cities grew bigger. As more settlers arrived, pioneers began moving westward, cutting and chopping their way across a wilderness of wooded hills and tree-covered mountains.

When they reached the western coast, they found endless stands of giant trees. They felt uncomfortable in this darkly dense landscape. Like the earlier settlers, they thought they owned the land to use as they pleased. They began cutting down the ancient trees, once more clearing and burning, and now selling the wood for lumber.

Our Sitka spruce continued to grow in spite of these loggers and fires. It was surrounded by an old forest, later protected as parkland – all because there were a few insightful people who loved the wilderness and devoted great effort to preserving its beauty.

Time continued. As the world turned, the climate
changed. The air was no longer filled with birds, nor the
sea with salmon. Industry spewed out sludge and smoke,
dimming even the stars. Sprawling cities and speeding
highways paved over the freshness of farmland.
Whole forests disappeared.

All creation was smeared and smudged and
dirtied. What had become of the Earth's caretakers?
Where were they now? Men no longer tread lightly
on the land. They had forgotten that this Earth is our
only home and that its soil gives life to all that grows.
Even farmland was now sold for profit and development,
just as the forests had been.

But all the money in the world will not buy back
the birds or the salmon, or even one old-growth tree.

Today science teaches us that trees allow our planet to breathe. They cleanse both air and water, taking in carbon dioxide and giving back oxygen, drinking in ground water and returning sweet, clean moisture to the air. Trees provide shade and cooling to a planet fast becoming too warm. They hold precious soil and support a vast community of beneficial insects and wildlife. Old trees are able to refresh mankind and help restore harmony and balance to a dying world.

Violent storms, unexpected floods and terrible droughts were visited upon the Earth more often now. The coldest winter in memory came to the Pacific Northwest. Snow was shaken from the sky, swirling and spilling down until the forest was buried beneath the weight of it. Hidden wildlife trembled at the strange stillness in the air. All of Nature seemed to be holding its breath.

Then the trees began to freeze and crack, breaking the silent whiteness. Distant rumbling turned to a deafening roll of thunder. Lightening flickered and flashed, flaming out warning of what was to come. The wind awoke, its fury sweeping ocean waves into fountains of spray. Trees creaked and swayed, then snapped and splintered. Wintry blasts battered the towering spruce.

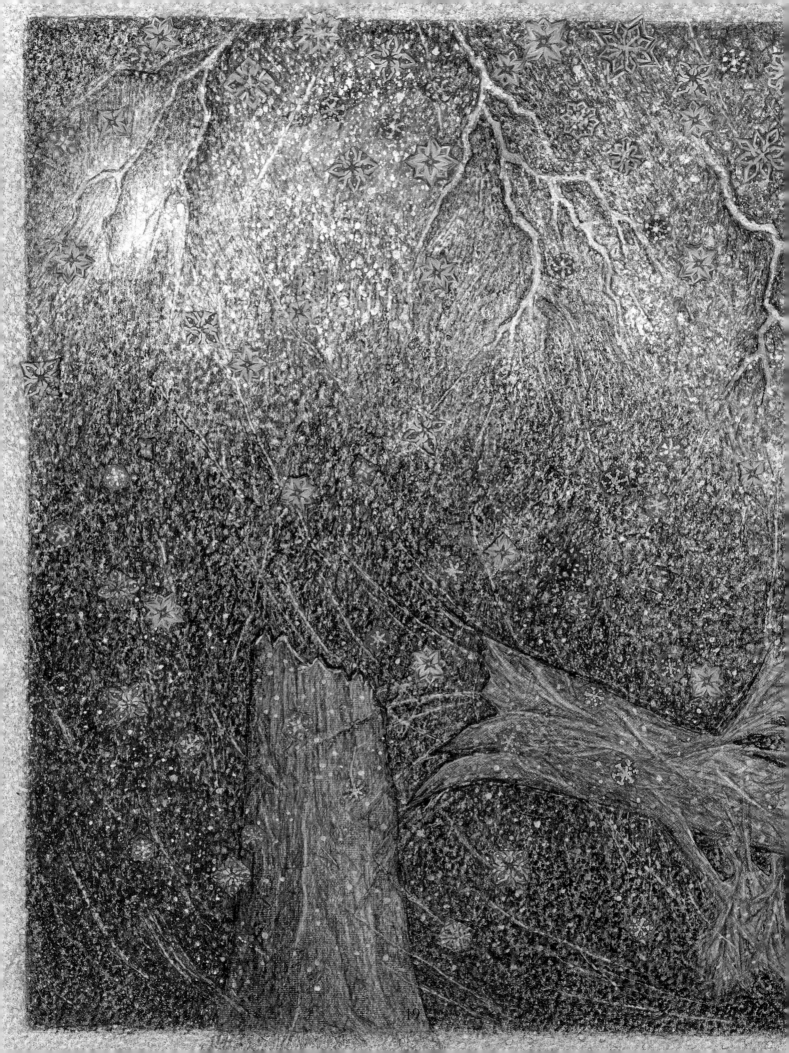

At last the ancient tree could bend no more.
It broke. Hundreds of years growing and now it fell
in a moment – crashing like a thunderbolt, shattering
the night, toppling every tree in its path, tearing apart
the forest tapestry. Terrified creatures scattered; the Earth
trembled and shook; the forest cried out its pain and loss
to the quaking darkness.

Nearby, in towns and cities, frightened people huddled without light or heat in the shelter of their homes. Only in the morning stillness did they begin to emerge, gathering quietly in small groups, studying the destruction that lay before them. Those who ventured into the woods were struck to the heart by the devastation and ruin. Their magnificent forest was torn apart, its spirit spent.

The song of the Sitka spruce had seemingly come
to an end, and in response the other trees were silent.
A hushed sorrow filled the air.

After many days of discussion and debate, those
in charge decided that the largest tree pieces should be
saved, some for lumber, some for firewood. The huge,
broken Sitka spruce would be kept for special use.

An unassuming instrument maker requested a piece to use
in crafting a cello. This man understood the forest and the trees.

He cherished this wood and studied his piece long and
carefully. He wished his instrument to be worthy of the
ancient tree. Season after season, he concentrated all his
skill and attention on making it so, his life's great work.

When at last the cello was complete, the instrument maker knew that he must return to the broken forest. There he sat on a tree stump, listening intently to the silent trees. Then he took out his cello and began to play, slowly and softly, like a quiet prayer. Touched once more by the sounds of the ancient wood, the trees responded, slowly and softly, their first small stirrings in harmony with the voice of the cello.

The instrument maker understood now that his work was well done and he was content. He would return often to these woods where his cello always played its most beautiful song, in tune with the heartbeat of the world. To him, the tender, whispered response of the trees was the greatest gift of all.

In spite of great loss and destruction,
Nature, deep down, is never spent.
The sound of beauty does not die.
Like the secret whispering song of
the trees, it will forever sing.
Pray that we may learn to listen.

Nature and Music Notes

By studying and observing nature, one sees how infinitely beautiful it is, how perfectly interconnected and complex.

A single tree is a living community, but also linked to all the world around it. The soil in which the tree is rooted is alive with worms, ants, insects, bugs, beetles, and micro-organisms. In an old-growth forest, half of the weight is beneath the ground. Tiny thread-like fungi reach everywhere through the earth, growing into the smallest rootlets, extending the tree's reach for food and moisture by one thousand times. They also connect the trees with one another, allowing them to communicate. When the soil is disturbed, the trees' connections to one another are broken.

It is miraculous that a tree may grow for century after century, then have its wood used to create an instrument that will be played for centuries more. Many of the world's finest string instruments were made in Cremona, Italy, as early as the mid 1500s. The wood came from nearby, from a very ancient forest. Some musicians say that Stradivari instruments always play their very best in the hills near Cremona. Perhaps this is because of a connection between the wood of the instrument and the living wood of the forest.

Paganini believed that Stradivari chose his wood from trees where nightingales sang. The nightingale (p. 22) is not found on our Sitka spruce. The following birds, however, were at one time found in the forests of the Pacific Northwest and are illustrated on these pages: bald eagle, great blue heron, great horned owl, raven and crow; hairy woodpecker, red-breasted sapsucker, Stellar's jay, varied thrush, and brown creeper; purple finch, chestnut-backed chickadee, nuthatch, Pacific-slope flycatcher, pine siskin, and golden-crowned kinglet. The short-tailed albatross, glaucous-winged and herring gulls were once found along the coastal forests.

Also pictured are: the black bear, deer, porcupine, racoon, red squirrel, pine marten, and vole. Not long ago, salmon also thrived in the coastal waters.

For more information, references, and teaching notes, please see www.hestewart.com

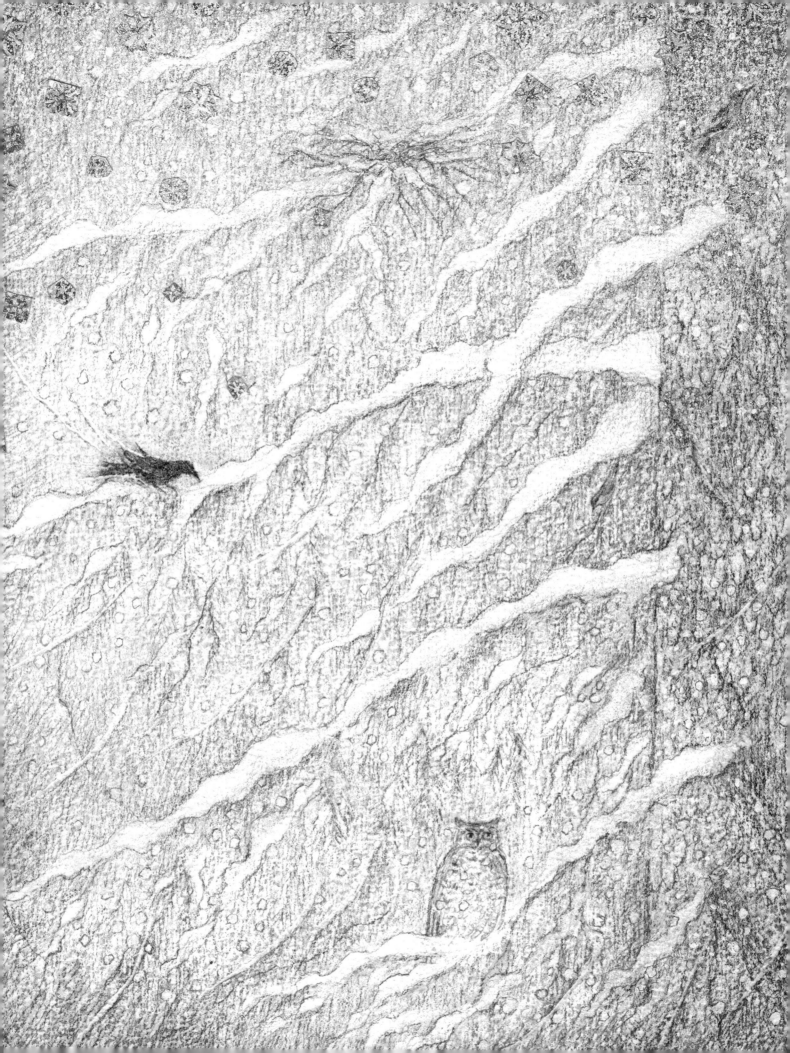